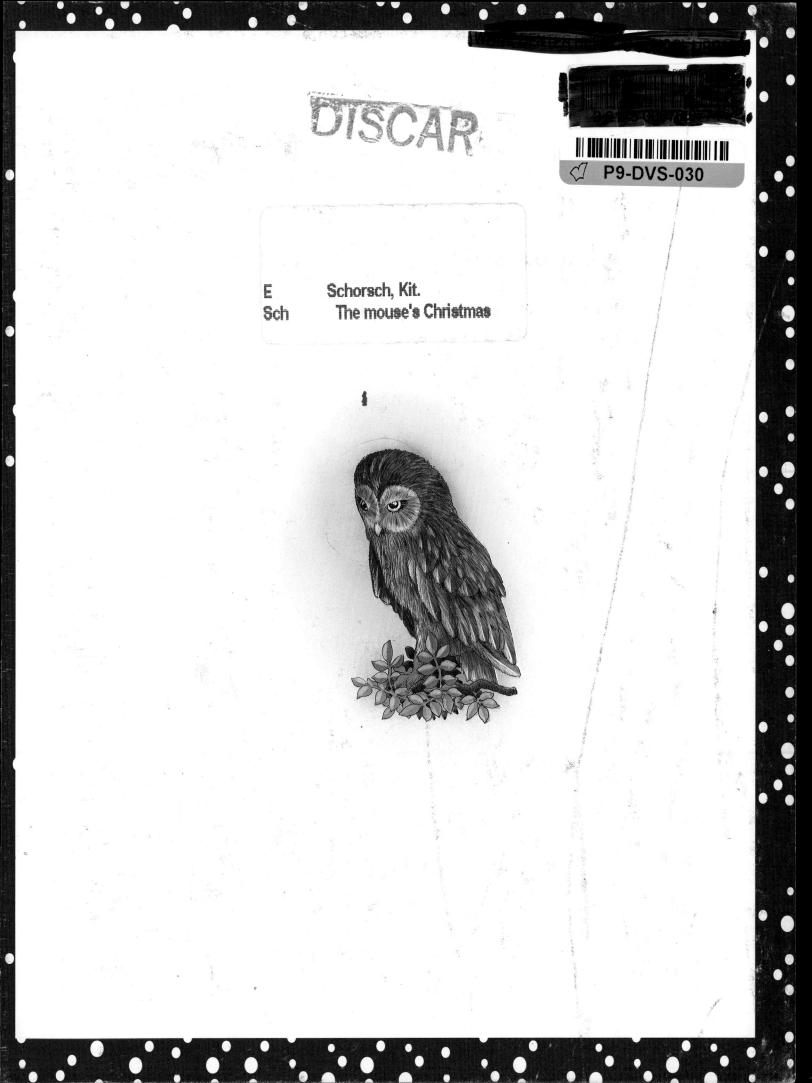

© Aladdin Books Ltd 1996
© Text and illustrations Alan Baker 1996

Designed and produced by
Aladdin Books Ltd
28 Percy Street
London W1P 0LD

First published in the United States in 1996 by
Copper Beech Books
an imprint of
The Millbrook Press
2 Old New Milford Road
Brookfield, Connecticut 06804

Designed by
David West Children's Book Design

Library of Congress Cataloging-in-Publication Data
Baker, Alan.
Mouse's Christmas / by Alan Baker.
p. cm.
Summary: When Mouse visits each of his friends as they busily
prepare for Christmas, he wonders if they have forgotten about
him - until he finds a surprise awaiting him at home.
ISBN 0-7613-0503-3
[1. Mice–Fiction. 2. Animals–Fiction. 3. Christmas–Fiction.]
I. Title
PZ7.B1688Mo   1996
[E]–dc20
96-2332   CIP   AC

Printed in Singapore

Mouse's Christmas

Alan Baker

COPPER BEECH BOOKS

BROOKFIELD, CONNECTICUT

Outside, it is a cold Christmas Eve. Mouse hasn't
seen any of his friends for days. He decides to visit them all.

"Merry Christmas Mouse," Badger calls back,
but he's resting and doesn't get up.

Outside, Mouse shivers with cold. He sets off on the long
journey over the hills to visit the foxes' house.

Inside, the foxes
Christmas dinne

"Merry Christmas Mouse," they reply hurriedly and carry
on with their mixing and baking.

Outside, it is getting colder. Mouse decides to try the rabbits.
He quickly scampers off down the path through the woods.

When he gets to the rabbits' door he calls out hopefully,
  "Merry Christmas Rabbits."

Inside, the rabbits are enjoying themselves, busily blowing up balloons and hanging the last of their Christmas decorations.

"Merry Christmas Mouse," they cry back happily, but they don't stop what they are doing or invite Mouse inside.

Outside, it is beginning to snow.

"Perhaps Owl will have time to talk to me," Mouse thinks as he hurries on to where Owl lives.

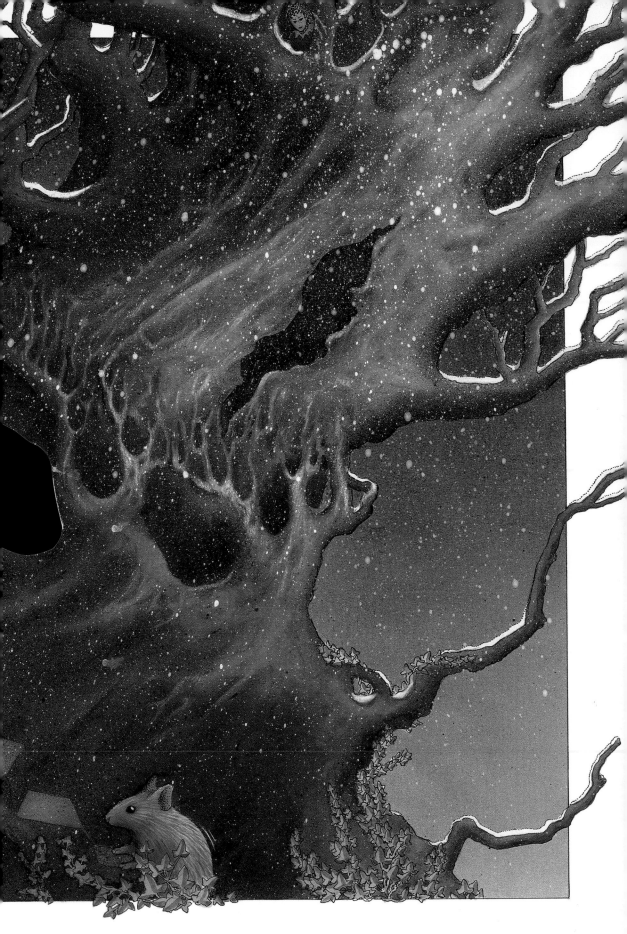

Mouse slowly climbs the many steps that wind up
Owl's tree.

Inside, Mouse finds that Owl is about to go out.
"Merry Christmas Owl," sighs Mouse sadly.
"Merry Christmas little Mouse," hoots Owl.

"I have to deliver this present to a very special friend,"
he says. "It's cold and late. Let me give you a ride home."

By now the snow is falling thick and fast.
Mouse climbs carefully onto Owl's back and holds on tightly.
They fly off together into the night.

The snow lies deep on the ground. Down below, Mouse sees trail upon trail of footprints leading to his door.

"Who can be visiting me at this time of night?" he wonders.

Inside Mouse's house the fire is lit, the tree is decorated, and all his friends are waiting there for him with lots of presents. "Surprise, surprise!" they cry out. "Merry Christmas Mouse."

So no one was actually too busy for Mouse after all -
and certainly none of his friends had forgotten him.
This really is a very special Mouse's Christmas!